MATILDA
and the
DRAGON

JULIAN BURNSIDE
ILLUSTRATED BY
BETTINA GUTHRIDGE

A LITTLE ARK BOOK

ALLEN & UNWIN

To Katherine, with love. J.W.K.B.
And Oscar, with thanks. B.B.G.

First published 1991

A Little Ark Book
Allen & Unwin Pty Ltd
8 Napier Street, North Sydney, NSW 2059, Australia

National Library of Australia
Cataloguing-in-Publication entry:

Burnside, Julian.
    Matilda and the dragon.

    ISBN 1 86373 127 X.
    ISBN 1 86373 144 X.
    1. Children's poetry, Australian. I. Guthridge,
    Bettina. II. Title.

A821.3

Designed by Sandra Nobes
Set in Baskerville by Bookset
Printed by South Wind Production, Singapore

A little girl, known as Matilda,
Took a trip that nearly killed her!

She was supposed to be in bed,
But couldn't sleep, or so she said.
She crept unseen into the night,
Causing great distress and fright.

She scampered off towards the bus,
And didn't think of all the fuss
She'd cause by going off alone—
She didn't write, she didn't phone.

She ran to where the buses leave,
And saw a sight you won't believe.
It made Matilda gasp and stare—
The bus stop was no longer there!

Instead, there was a gaping hole
From which emerged a shiny pole
(The sort for sliding firemen down,
To fight a fire in the town).

Matilda saw the pole and thought,
'This looks like fun; but still, I ought
To touch the bottom with my toe
To test its depth. Well here we go . . .'

She reached right in and groped around,
Her fingers clinging to the ground.
'This hole is deeper than a well,'
Matilda thought—then in she fell!

Imagine poor Matilda's plight,
Plunging down into the night.
Spiders looked at her, surprised—
They thought her antics ill-advised.

Now, what Matilda wished to know
Was how far down the hole would go.
'Perhaps I've been a bit unwise,'
She thought. But then, a great surprise—

The pole was gone, don't ask me where,
And she was falling through the air,
Hurtling down to fields of green,
Towards a giant trampoline!

She landed flat and bounced up high,
Did perfect back-flips in the sky.
Somersaults and pirouettes she did with grace and style
But then she stopped and looked about, and noticed with a smile . . .

That all around, the fields she saw
Were made of emeralds, and, what's more,
Toffee trees with chocolate leaves,
And giant licorice sticks in sheaves.

Just then she saw a wondrous thing—
Right by the woods, all sleek and fat,
Lounging, languid, playing cards,
A giant, smoking dragon sat.

She thought at first that she should hide,
For dragons can be awfully mean.
But then she thought she'd like a ride—
And, anyway, she'd just been seen!

The dragon raised his scaly head,
Looked at Matilda, roared and said,
'I'm going to take you home for tea.
Why don't you come along with me?'

Matilda got a dreadful fright.
She screamed and ran around a lot.
She hurtled off around a corner—
Straight into the dragon's pot!

A ghastly spot, you'll understand,
Without a friend to lend a hand.
Experience so far had taught her
Not to get into hot water!

Just then the dragon sprang at her,
Exclaiming, 'Hiss, gawhizzle, whirr!'

But did he eat her? He did not.
He lifted her straight from the pot

And said, 'Oh goodness, dearie me,
When I invited you to tea
I wanted you to dine *with* me,
You weren't supposed to *be* the tea!!'

The dragon showed Matilda round
His jewelled cave, without a sound.
Amidst the gloom and smoky swirls
Were chests of diamonds, gold and pearls,

Emeralds and amethyst, ivory and jade,
Books and maps and candlesticks and rugs of silken braid;
Cakes and scones and french eclairs
And jugs of lemonade!

Matilda said, 'I'm glad we're friends,
Our time has just begun.
Let's find out where the rainbow ends,
Let's go and chase the sun!'

The dragon showed her how to fly.
They flew into the darkening sky.
They found a fun fair in the park
And rode the rocket train 'til dark.

They went together, hand in hand,
And built a castle in the sand.
And then they walked along the beach,
Finding shells and trying to teach
The moonbeams how to dance on waves;
Exploring secret, hidden caves.

They found a tunnel, dark and deep,
With roof so low they had to creep
Until they saw a glint of light,
And then they got a frightful fright.

They found they were beneath the sea,
And peered into the inky dark:
A pale gray fin, gigantic fangs,
The cold shape of a jawsome shark!

Matilda screamed, the dragon too—
Where could they go, what could they do?
Then Dragon took a mighty breath,
Blew flames, and fried the shark to death!

'Good,' said the dragon, 'Great,' said he,
'Now we'll have fish and chips for tea!'

They started tea, but as they did
Down swooped a slithering, slimy squid.

Matilda jumped on Dragon's back
Before the squid had time to think.
The dragon ran, the squid gave chase
And squirted clouds of thick black ink!

They swam into a cave and hid,
And finally escaped the squid.
Then Dragon's footstep made a 'squish'—
He'd trodden on a jellyfish!

'Yuk!' said Matilda, 'Did it sting?'
'Yes!' said Dragon from the swing,
Which hung down near the cavern door
Where Dragon leapt to rub his paw.

They kept on walking through the caves,
Then looking up they saw the waves,
Which meant that they could swim for shore,
And so they swam, and swam some more.

However hard Matilda tried,
She couldn't swim against the tide.
The dragon picked her up and said,
'Why don't you ride upon my head?'

And so she sat between his ears,
As in they surfed, to noisy cheers
Of people, strolling on the sand,
Who stopped to stare and lend a hand.

Then, as she leapt off Dragon's head,
Matilda heard a voice which said:
'Your magic world is not a dream,
But things aren't always what they seem.'

Matilda swooned and all went black.
She woke up lying on her back
In bed. And there her Father found her,
Knelt, and put his arms around her,
Saying softly, 'Did you scream?
You must have had a dreadful dream.'

Matilda smiled, held out her hand,
And guess what—it was full of sand!